Lâu Tsí-û

Not Your Child

劉芷妤

別人的孩子

Not Your Child
Lâu Tsí-û

Translated by Jenna Tang

First published in English by Strangers Press, Norwich, 2024
Part of UEA Publishing Project

All rights reserved
Author © Lâu Tsí-û, 2024
Translator © Jenna Tang, 2024

Printed by
Swallowtail, Norwich

Series editors
Nathan Hamilton
Jeremy Tiang

Cover design and typesetting
Glen & Rebecca Robinson (www.glenandrebecca.com)

Design Copyright © 2024
Glen Robinson, Rebecca Robinson

The rights of Lâu Tsí-û to be identified as the author and Jenna Tang to be identified as the translator of this work have been asserted in accordance with the Copyright, Designs and Patents Act, 1988. This booklet is sold subject to the condition that it shall not, by way of trade or otherwise, be lent, resold, hired out, stored in a retrieval system, or otherwise circulated without the publisher's prior consent in any form of binding or cover other than that in which it is published and without a similar condition including this condition being imposed on the subsequent purchaser.

ISBN: 978-1-915812-66-7

ká-sióng was made possible through generous funding from the Ministry of Culture, Taiwan; National Museum of Taiwan Literature; and Literature from Taiwan.

NOT YOUR CHILD
LÂU TSÍ-Û

TRANSLATED BY JENNA TANG

別人的孩子

AT RUSH HOUR ON A FRIDAY, the crowds swarming public transportation were like the wandering spirits of Ghost Month, snatching offerings from crowded dedication tables. Actually no, even wandering spirits of Good Brothers have to take a few clumsy steps back to let all these people by. And, thinking about it, there is a Friday every week, whereas Ghost Month is annual, so in fact it wasn't at all comparable to these humans' day-to-day.

Why can't these people hurry up and die? They would occupy less space as ghosts. Yu-Jie, who was quite short herself, standing at less than 150cm tall, was pushed and jostled as she squeezed out of the MRT carriage. Partly out of resentment at her diminutive stature, she exaggeratedly rolled her eyes, briefly resembling a dead fish, before flipping them back into place, and it was hard to tell whether her nostrils were flared due to extreme irritation or a desperate need for fresh air. She focussed all her anger and resentment out through her nose.

別人的孩子
NOT YOUR CHILD

It was also hard to tell whose among the crowd's nostrils spewed the most resentment. But Yu-Jie hoped the air *she* spewed might cling as curses to those strangers whom she thought especially merited them. She wanted these curses to linger and dwell in them.

The phone she was clutching in her right hand began to ring. It was so crowded she couldn't raise it to answer right away. She strained and struggled to turn her wrist to flip her phone to check, deep at arm's length.

It was indeed her manager.

"Fuck your pussy!" Was the reward on finally being able to raise her phone to her ear in answer.

"Where the fuck are you, Chou Yu-Jie? Facebook is exploding and you're doing nothing? All the phones are ringing like crazy, nobody has the time to answer them for you, get it?"

As managing the Facebook page was one of her duties, Yu-Jie had indeed been aware that the inboxes were overflowing for some time. Notifications were coming in so quickly it would have been hard for anyone not to notice, and certainly too many to keep up. She'd had no choice but to turn them off so her phone wouldn't keep buzzing, to preserve her battery for when it mattered.

"I'm on it, but there are too many messages, they just keep coming... Agh!" She tripped as she herded along with the crowd toward the stairs. She felt guilty, and swallowed a further mouthful of swelling curses down to her stomach. It was like gulping down vomit before it could fully erupt. The thought made Yu-Jie involuntarily retch and gag.

"Do your fucking job... what? Are you vomitting?"

"Not at you, boss," she slowed down, "I'm sorry, but I... as you know, I am on leave — I applied a month and a half ago, so..."

"Fuck your balls! What? Leave? You're on *leave* today?" Her manager already seemed so agitated you'd have thought his rear end was in flames; but now it was as if the mention of leave had caused him to grow a second ass, which was now also on fire.

劉芷妤
LÂU TSÍ-Û

"Where the hell are you right now?"

According to Yu-Jie's request, which had been accepted, she should've left the constituency office early this morning. *If it wasn't for all these constant emergencies, I wouldn't be departing so late in the first place...* But though Yu-Jie was usually very direct, she was aware that this probably wasn't the best time to say these things out loud. *How many times would I die if I just said it? I'd be so dead I wouldn't even become a ghost... I would be more dead than even the dead. And I wouldn't ever get to enjoy all the offerings. How miserable.*

"Um I um, I'm here at the train station..." Before she'd been able to finish, her phone was knocked clear of her hand as someone shoved her while trying to squeeze past.

"My phone!" Yu-Jie watched it tumble and then slide out of the MRT gate. She couldn't bear this day anymore. She turned toward the culprit, a man in black shirt, trainers, and jeans, and shouted, "What the *fuck* is your problem?! Watch where you're going, you fucking dick. I can't even tap through the gate now!"

"You walk too slowly. My son couldn't get past. He hardly bumped you at all, it's your own fault for not holding onto your phone properly."

Ah, it was his kid who bumped into me, that makes more sense. I'm the height of a hobbit, the man's arm would just have passed over the top of my head.

"Miss, your phone..."

Another man, his tone and expression much kinder and more considerate, handed it back over the gate. It was such a pleasant contrast, this sudden, unexpected gesture; it briefly assuaged her mounting desire to destroy the entire world.

On retrieving her phone, she was ready to express something bullshit like how could she ever reward his immense kindness with her life, maybe even hold his gaze a little longer than necessary, but the kind man had already turned away, taking his girlfriend by the hand as he left.

别人的孩子
NOT YOUR CHILD

Alright, fuck the world.

Her phone wasn't broken, it seemed, at least; she apparently hadn't wasted her money on the expensive, anti-collision case. But her call with her manager had ended. She wasn't sure if that was due to the bump or her manager's having finally combusted entirely. Assuming he hadn't, she would have to call back and apologise.

She exited the MRT gates and proceeded toward the high-speed rail. She pressed "call back" but the call kept failing. Utterly frustrated, she lifted her head, only to find a familiar frowning face on the silent LCD screen above the walkway through a gap in the crowd, popping up on the news.

"It's not enough to keep talking about increasing penalties. That would only resolve the issue temporarily, but the root cause of the problem would still be there. It might even lead to more problems..." Yu-Jie instinctively murmured the words with which the MP had so enflamed the public at the precise moment her manager chose to pick up the call, causing him to rain down further curses: "Are you taking the piss? Don't we have enough to deal with?"

The screen was showing footage of the midday press conference where the argument had arisen. The reason she was able to identify these words right away wasn't because this scene had been replayed hundreds of times within a few hours, but because it was, regrettably, she who had drafted the speech.

"So sorry, I just happened to see another news replay..."

"I don't care. Get back here right away. Fuck, otherwise..."

Yu-Jie had finally arrived at the gate. She tilted her head to clamp her phone to her shoulder as her hands groped for her ticket in her slouchy shoulder bag. She hadn't been able to find it by the time she reached the gate, and so quickly moved to the side to be out of anyone's way — then she realised her ticket was saved in her phone.

"... Hey hey boss, give me a sec, just one sec..." She lowered her phone and swiped a few times, until the QR code appeared. She

劉芷妤
LÂU TSÍ-Ú

then pushed back into the crowd, half-squeezing and half-standing-in-line to scan. Just as she was about to tuck her phone back to her ear to resume the call, another notification flashed up on her screen: "Auntie, are you coming home today? You promised."

"Oh no…" A menacing energy behind her ribcage gripped her heart. She clutched her phone, trying to contain the anxiety that felt like it might explode from her chest, reminding herself that on the other end of the phone was an angry old octopus frantically waving its flaming tentacles. She stuffed her phone back to her ear.

"Hey, I'm very sorry, boss, I really have to…"

"You *have* to come back, that's what you *have* to do! Shit, don't you understand? Madame Mazu herself is in for a meeting later, and everyone will be on their own stuff after — while you, you're just dicking around? What the fuck?" Be they assistants at the parliament office or at the constituency office, whenever someone spoke about the MP privately, they tended to call her Madame Mazu after the compassionate and motherly goddess of the same name and the patronising, matronly image she liked to foster for herself. The way she went about things, she generally lived up to the image.

"No, I really have to travel back south right now. I'm very sorry boss, but…"

"What's so damn important you're off to do in the south? We're all about to start our meeting and you're heading… where exactly? Are you fucking off to eat ghost food?"

"Can't you just send me the minutes? I'll be able to write up a full statement in half an hour. Or fifteen minutes if it's time-sensitive, it doesn't matter where I am. I don't have to be in the office."

"Doesn't matter my ass, even if it takes a fart's worth of time to finish the draft, if you're not physically with us, even if Madame Mazu says nothing, all of your colleagues will be pissed at you. Get your fucking ass back here. What the hell is so important you have to go back now, in the middle of all this?"

Why would I have to go back now?

别人的孩子
NOT YOUR CHILD

Yu-Jie could see she was not in an advantageous position. Flames of potential anger were unable to flare. All she could do was murmur apologies and avoid the question. She whispered a series of 'sorry's as she passed through a scattering crowd on the escalator, trying to make it to her train before the doors closed. She had reserved a ticket she couldn't use in the end. *Just get on the train before anything else happens.*

Like every rush hour, the unreserved carriages got so crowded that some people were piled almost onto the overhead luggage rack. Yu-Jie didn't expect to find a seat but glimpsed one through a crowd of backsides. She took advantage of being small and made her way through and sat herself down. It turned out that a man had just stood to lift his luggage up to the shelf while she had usurped his seat behind him. *You snooze, you lose.* After all, who could really claim an unreserved seat just because his butt had been there briefly before. The man stood aside, blew at his beard and glared at her, cursing under his breath. Yu-Jie pretended she'd seen nothing and turned toward the window to speak into the phone, but, with the darkness outside, there was no escaping his look of venomous resentment reflected in the window. Yu-Jie's mouth was again full of apologies, but now there was no way to tell if these apologies were for her manager or for the man in the mirror.

There's nothing I can do, this world is all about either letting someone else down or letting myself down.

In the end, her manager hung up, still cursing at her. She felt covered in shame, as though rivers of apology might stream from her nose, but she immediately called the message sender: Yinyin.

She wouldn't usually do so for anyone but she had secretly bought a mobile phone for Yinyin in order that they might be in touch. Yinyin's mother, Yu-Jie's older sister, Yu-Ping, didn't know about this phone; for her part, Yu-Jie didn't dare imagine what would happen if her sister, six years her elder, ever found out.

Yinyin wasn't picking up. *Was it because nothing had really*

劉芷妤
LÂU TSÍ-Û

happened, or because she simply wasn't able? If the latter, was it because she was in some kind of danger, or was she simply being cautious so as not to let her mother find out about her phone? She had begun to spiral with such thoughts.

She hung up and called Yu-Ping.

Again, nobody picked up.

Calm down, just calm down.

Yu-Jie intentionally slowed down her motions, stuffing her bag under her seat and closing her legs above it. She pressed her phone against her lap with both hands and took a deep breath, letting her diaphragm sink down a little, helping to calm her mind. It was a technique she had learned when following the MP to vocal training. It was important to learn how to breathe, something that can be controlled.

Shit, I almost forgot — the course!

There had been a lot of abuse online claiming the MP's voice was "*So high-pitched, so squeaky when she debates in the council, and she sounds so emotional; she makes absolutely no sense… Nobody gets this bitch…,*" etc and so while the team continued perusing laws and clauses, gathering research, they also thought it might be a good idea if she could please undergo three hours of vocal training courses on Friday nights, just to strengthen her position. The course was arranged with the help of an old acquaintance of Yu-Jie's who used to work at a professional theatre and Yu-Jie had taken charge of making contact but had forgotten to inform her friend they might have to cancel today's session, what with events.

Yu-Jie held her phone out in front of her, her thumbs quickly typing on the screen. The man next to the window suddenly spread open his evening newspaper, his arms stretched wide as though unaware anyone was sitting next to him. Once again, Yu-Jie's phone was knocked to the floor.

Oh sure, pile it on. Maybe a few more things could go wrong today, please? Thanks.

别人的孩子
NOT YOUR CHILD

"Oh, excuse me."

Beneath the newspaper, his exposed thighs spread from his shorts as wide as the newspaper pages — comfortably, freely, he spread his wings and went on flying as his apology drifted above her head like a wisp of cloud. Yu-Jie, on the other hand, bent to retrieve her phone in discomforted embarrassment.

So self-satisfied. He must have a successful career. A happy family.

It took her a while to find her way tactfully between the man's legs to, with some effort, delicately retrieve her phone. She straightened up, planning to ask him to be more mindful of the people around him. But she froze as she caught sight of the photo on the front page of the newspaper: again, the midday press conference with the MP alongside the victim's family. The girl's grandparents, uncles and aunties were all kneeling on the ground, and, standing next to them, the MP — who clearly hadn't expected they would actually kneel in front of her — had been caught as a result with a particularly contorted facial expression that inadvertently expressed disgust.

Above the photo was a piercing headline:

Lolita Rape Case Revelation! Evil Wolf Was Cousin?

The train jolted, then started to move.

It had all exploded the day before, as the parliamentary session was coming to an end. Yu-Jie, who had assisted at the meeting, had studiously ticked off everything on her to-do list with extra efficiency so she might start her leave sooner. She was packing to head back south the next morning, as news of a little girl having been savagely attacked at her elementary school starting breaking, bringing with it the usual distasteful storms of criticism and public opinion on the internet; and, given the subject matter, the flames of public fury burned so fiercely this time it seemed hell itself might engulf the mortal world.

劉芷妤
LÂU TSÍ-Û

Why can't humans simply live their days happily? Why must we make our own hell? What must the ghosts think of us.

The attacker had been subdued, by a number of adults who had been at the elementary school yard early to exercise, before he could harm any others. At that point it was thought that thankfully none of the children had been harmed and only a few adults had been lightly hurt while apprehending the culprit. Later, though, they discovered a little girl inside who had gone to the bathroom alone earlier and who had apparently been wounded by the criminal as he passed by. She was immediately sent to the ER.

The little girl had been found unconscious, having lost a lot of blood, and with her trousers having been torn open. Public outcry had spread like wildfire. School security, public stabbings, penalties for sexual assault of minors, connections between reduced sentences, mental health, even abolishing the death penalty — all were fuel to a wildfire hunger for justice spreading across the land. It spread without logic, evidence or reason as a horrified rage that might yet burn everything to ashes.

The little girl's school happened to be in their MP's electoral district, so the moment they had left the parliamentary meeting they received the manager's call briefly summarising the incident and confirming that the girl's family was willing to accept a visit from the MP. The manager had then also asked the MP and Yu-Jie to head straight to the hospital to express their concern. She accompanied the MP to the hospital. On their way, she quickly scanned the major news reports, comments, and social feeds. The little girl remained unconscious, the criminal had already been sentenced and in some cases executed by the online public myriad times.

When they arrived at the hospital, nurses were pumping a blood transfusion in an attempt to save the girl's life. The girl's father worked in the mainland, so he wasn't able to make it back right away; her mother had cried so hard she'd fainted a few times; the grandparents, uncles, and aunties living across the street were

别人的孩子
NOT YOUR CHILD

out of their minds with indignation, expressing to the MP that the perpetrator needed to be severely punished. The wounds on the girl's face might be permanent, it might affect her future marriage prospects, they said. Not to mention this was sexual assault of a minor. This was the destruction of the lifelong innocence of a woman, and as such it must not be tolerated by a decent society such as ours!

That was when the MP proposed a Sexual Assault Crime Prevention Act, which was being discussed and studied carefully, while the family of the little girl presented themselves in front of microphones and cameras, desperately pleading with the MP to include severe punishments such as whipping, scalding, chemical castration, and no parole, so this unconscionable criminal would receive proper punishment.

Having seen the state of the little girl and met with her heartbroken mother, the MP and Yu-Jie had both been deeply affected. But Yu-Jie also knew very clearly that amending the law in such a way was potentially dangerous and went against Madame Mazu's fundamental ideology. In the end, the MP didn't agree to anything on the spot, instead equivocating and expressing she would do her best to provide any possible help for the girl and her family.

Of course, such vague phrasing wasn't at all helpful or acceptable to a family in distress and nor was it in the eyes of the preying media, and internet. They attacked the MP as being perfunctory, putting on a show, and hypocritically for using someone else's hurt for her own, in this case, political gain. This wasn't the first such incident in the news. In some ways, though unpredictable in its specifics, it all could have been predicted before a single thing had been uttered at all; the words spoken, the consequences of those words. Yu-Jie, standing on the side, had advised the MP to let the family take the lead, but the MP hadn't changed her tack.

Yu-Jie understood the MP's concerns: she was unwilling to speak against her own principles, but didn't want to upset the family

劉芷妤
LÂU TSÍ-Û

further by openly opposing their position in a difficult moment through taking the moral high ground. In the end, the MP said all that she could say.

  Deep down, however, Yu-Jie was more on the family's side. That is, even though Yu-Jie worked closely with the MP and shared many of her political convictions, whenever incidents of sexual harassment or sexual assault arose, she found it hard to support the MP's perspective of moral relativism — or perhaps what she couldn't abide was how someone who had never been hurt directly by these issues could dismiss such a topic so lightly; or perhaps she resented herself, for not having that luxury; or her brother, who had taken it away from her.

  But Yu-Jie also knew the MP wasn't the way everyone described her. She shouldn't even be thinking this way, but, at such moments, even she couldn't help but feel a bit of hatred towards a woman who was unable to fully deal with a situation like this. Did these things not matter simply because this was not her child?

  In the taxi back to the office, Yu-Jie had remained silent. At the beginning, she had no idea whether the MP was aware of how upset she was with her. She had simply leaned back in her seat and closed her eyes. As for Yu-Jie, she frantically swiped her phone, becoming so frustrated by all the cursing and criticism in the process that tears dropped from her eyes. What really pierced her were comments like: "Because she never had her own children, she will never fully understand this heartbreak; she thinks other people's children can just go and die."

She's not like that! She's Madame Mazu. She has deep empathy!
Yu-Jie was no longer even sure why she was crying, or for whom.
How could Gender Education be the top priority right now? So many little boys and girls were harmed. After your Sex Education, how many others would you sacrifice? Why wouldn't you tie these sons of bitches together and grind them into ashes and drop them into the sea?

  As they were about to reach the office, the MP, with her eyes

别人的孩子
NOT YOUR CHILD

still closed, said: "Yu-Jie, stop swiping at your phone. It's so dark in the car, it will hurt your eyes as well as your heart."

By the time they stepped into the office, things had taken a horrible turn.

The little girl was still unconscious, but they had now found signs of sexual assault. But they weren't recent. These were old wounds.

The kid sitting behind Yu-Jie hadn't been able to keep still, so he stood up and looked around. Out of boredom, he again read out the newspaper headline, word by word. "Daddy, what does that mean? How are cousins wolves? Do they transform during a full moon?"

"Aiya, you can't understand, not now, don't read that out loud." His father became awkward, but he sounded oddly familiar. Yu-Jie took a peek through the gap between the seats. The same father and son from the subway gate.

"Huh? I didn't read it wrong. It was written that way, why would that girl's cousin become an evil wolf? I want to be a werewolf, too! Werewolves are cool! Can I be a good wolf?" Yu-Jie couldn't help but giggle.

"There's no such thing as a good wolf, not in that way — that kind of wolf is evil, and you won't become one, don't worry."

"Huh? But I, *want* to, why not —"

"Aiyo, I said no — please drop it."

The father was so embarrassed that people around them started to chuckle. A middle-aged woman who'd been standing in the corridor came to his rescue. She said to the father, "Kids say whatever comes into their little heads, adorable."

"Yeah, I don't know what his mother's been teaching him. Is she trying to frame me?! Ha!"

"Kids are like blank paper, innocent and harmless, it doesn't reflect on you."

劉芷妤
LÂU TSÍ-Û

The woman sitting next to the father said, "You're caring for your kid alone? That's so much work."

"Nah, it's just what I should be doing. His mother is at the Ghost Month Festival event, at the temple she couldn't take him, school is out, so here I am. But yeah, it's so much work, I wish I could just knock him out sometimes."

"There's not a lot of good men nowadays." The woman continued. "Your wife is really lucky."

Then there were two cases instead of one and every few hours they took another drastic turn. The arguments and discussions were unable to keep up with the speed and precipitous range of these turns, ready as they were at any stage to plunge straight down the mountainous valley. Finally, this morning, Yu-Jie had almost made it to the train station when a call from her manager forced her back to the office with all her luggage in tow.

The reason: after the little girl woke up, she had told the hospital staff that her trousers were unzipped because she had been about to pee when she was attacked. After some time with the hospital staff, trying to get the little girl to pour her heart out, she also revealed that she would play "adult games" with herself from time to time. The person from whom she had learned this game of trying to put all kinds of objects into her body was her older cousin, who lived across the street and who would be attending junior high school in the fall.

Once they heard that the culprit was their beloved, golden grandson who would one day inherit the family's wealth, the grandparents, uncles and aunties — who had chased the MP and Yu-Jie out of the hospital in front of all the major media the night before — then, without discussing it with the victim's mother, had rushed to the constituency office, strongly expressing they

别人的孩子
NOT YOUR CHILD

supported a preventive principle of "education instead of severe punishment." They also said they were hoping to officially state their new perspective in front of the press.

It was after this that the MP had started to draw all the fire.

Kids aren't merely blank paper. She resisted the impulse to turn her head and shoo away their platitudes. She knew they were just saying this like everybody else, rather than through any proper thinking. *Kids aren't blank paper, they are human beings with their own bodies and organs, they have desires that blank paper doesn't.*

And you can't just blame TV. Before smartphones, iPads, and the like, blank paper already knew how to sneak into his younger sister's room at midnight, how to reach his hand under her quilt, snake into his sister's panties.

Yu-Jie held her phone, and with all her heart, fought the moisture that welled up behind her eyeballs. She disliked all body fluids, wherever they came from; she also disliked crying; what she had learnt in the parliament office was a common lesson: when men cried, they were revealing their true feelings; when women cried, they were being hysterical.

Different genders have different liquids; some that look the same, and others that flowed between a deep sociological divide.

It started when Yu-Jie was eight years old. Yu-Tang, her fourteen-year-old brother, would even complain that she didn't know "how to get wet, so I can't even put it in." Yu-Tang's twin, Yu-Ping, would lay right beside Yu-Jie, pretending she knew nothing. She hated her brother's as well as her own; she loathed fluids that flowed from the upper body, as well as those from the lower parts.

The victim in this case was only ten years old.

And Yinyin, who was waiting for her in their hometown in the south, was nine.

劉芷妤
LÂU TSÍ-Û

Yu-Jie swiped her phone and still saw no messages in response. She sent another.

Her vision began to blur.

By now, the train had stopped and people on the platform, like sticky bobas being poured through a funnel, squeezed through the doors, then rolled into the carriage in clumps. There were barely any gaps between them, more crowded than the offerings on a Ghost Month table. Several rows away a woman was streaming a video clip that had gone viral on social media, something edited and cut by a few users. Half the carriage was able to hear, at manipulated volumes and speeds, the MP speaking in a ridiculous, laughable duck voice, screechy and monotonous, calling for earlier sex education — stop instilling the concept of chastity in their kids, so when kids were violated, they wouldn't feel they had to keep their mouths shut out of shame or guilt, so these kids wouldn't blame themselves for not having protected their precious virtue, so the idea of chastity wouldn't become an excuse for criminals to threaten children or for children to feel they had to cover up such sinful deeds.

Hahahahaha, precious virtue. Hahahahaha, guilt. Hahahahaha. She even wants to teach kids how not to feel ashamed.

Though the strange sounds and tones in the video were full of irony, most passengers around the woman had disgusted expressions on their faces and discussed the matter openly, both loudly or quietly. Meanwhile, Yu-Jie's eyes began to feel dry — perhaps because, from last night to this very moment, she had been repeatedly reading and listening to the same news reports, in their hundreds, each of which resembled one another; perhaps because, since the incident yesterday, to when she'd finally caught this train, she'd been by the side of the MP, speaking at length with the victim's mother and other family members, taking part in press conferences.

别人的孩子
NOT YOUR CHILD

The more she knew, the more she lost the sense of scalding, gossipy enthusiasm the general public still seemed to hold.

"How come this single, childless old hag gets to judge us? What does she mean sex education is more important than punishment? These people and their virtue-signalling! She doesn't even know how it feels to be a mother! She doesn't know what it means to carry a baby to full term — how giving birth to a baby is more painful than being hit by a car. Does she even know how hard it is to bring up a child in this world? She thinks other people's children can all die! Just because they're not her children!"

"Ha, she's old and ugly, and fierce, nobody's gonna marry her lah, she won't ever know what it is in this life, lah…"

"Such a bitch! Why isn't the girl's mother here? Surely she must be against all this nonsense."

The opinions expressed by this pair of bobas aligned more or less with the majority. During the press conference, even though what the MP had said was no different from what the grandparents, uncles and aunties had said themselves, because of manipulations in the mass media, most people's interpretation of this politically correct, even politically expedient, idea had somehow become politically incorrect. Everything was somehow ending up as the MP's responsibility alone. The image the MP had carefully promulgated, of being dedicated to protecting women's and children's rights, was being destroyed entirely. It somehow became, to some, evidence, even, of the opposite; she'd "finally dropped a fake, woke persona."

Not even half a day after the press conference, some of the media had started digging up the MP's personal history for special features; details of how many failed romances she'd supposedly had, that she appeared to have had a miscarriage, how she had longed to become a wife and mother, but nothing really came of it. How, in the end, all she could do was to plunge ahead with her political career to somehow "complete" her journey in life. Normally the staff would have laughed, dumbfounded, at something as inane as all this —

劉芷妤
LÂU TSÍ-Û

taking it seriously would just make the MP look bad, they didn't have the time to waste on such nonsense.

There was a stir a few rows in front of Yu-Jie. Then came a baby's intermittent crying, the clamour of luggage being moved, a young woman murmuring their thanks, and a teenage girl's loud "Thank you, uncles and aunties!" Yu-Jie puzzled together a warm moment of a woman with two kids accepting seats from kindly fellow passengers. Just like last night, when the victim's mother had held a little boy by her side. Mothers taking care of more than one child on their own always touched a corner of Yu-Jie's heart — she would remember her own mother. Her husband, Yu-Jie's father, had passed away from illness before Yu-Jie entered elementary school, so she'd had to bring up three kids alone. She always described her mother this way. There was nothing to doubt. And yet, she didn't know how to talk about how each of her mother's arms had held one of the twins, while Yu-Jie, so short, quiet, and shy, was often left out, or to one side.

Both her siblings had grown to average height, while Yu-Jie remained especially petite. A boy and a girl were already enough, so who is this hobbit? She felt worthless. Her mother had named the twins Yu-Tang and Yu-Ping — jade pavilion and jade artwork, a sign of her aspirations for them. Yu-Jie's name meant jade staircase; she felt more jaded than even jade itself, and certainly enough people were trampling over her.

She had never really shared these thoughts with anyone. It was hard enough for her mother, she didn't want to give her any more trouble than she had already. She didn't mention how her older brother had done all those late-night things to her every so often, not even after he entered a national university with such pride, but was later expelled because he had raped someone.

Even when their mother lay on her deathbed, she still lingered on the fact that Yu-Tang, after leaving university, had apparently just evaporated into thin air. Her brother had lost touch with them for years. Yu-Jie heard her mother, hovering between life and death,

別人的孩子
NOT YOUR CHILD

calling out Yu-Tang's name, over and over. She knew she had been right not to tell her anything.

The train began to advance again, the intermittent baby cries ahead grew louder. It was too crowded in the car, despite the AC. It felt like everyone had absorbed the hot air from outside and was now exhaling it into the car, all collaborating on a little pocket of hell.

Whenever Yu-Jie took public transit, she never felt fully human. Nobody else looked fully human to her, either. When human beings see many of the same things, our brains often merge them into a single entity, and so when, as politicos, we learn to view society as a whole, perhaps it's too easy to overlook individuals, treat people as if they are objects. Hard to see the trees from the demographic forest, so to speak. This was perhaps Madame Mazu's major failing. She could never get past this, and often found herself in direct conflict with a collective society, missing an individual or human connection, leading to her getting roasted, over and over, such as now, until she was blistered almost skinless.

Thinking about Madame Mazu made Yu-Jie instinctively glance at her phone. *They must be having that meeting by now.* It was she who had drafted the speech and, even though she'd based it on the MP's usual principles, the context had meant she'd ended up severely criticised for apparently defending the rights of sexual predators before those of anyone else. Yu-Jie started to feel a twinge of guilt about being absent. And fear. Never mind the MP, perhaps her colleagues might not understand her choices.

Even though she felt sorry, *very very sorry*.

But she'd had to go.

Yu-Jie's phone rang again. On the screen was the number of the family home. Her eyes widened. Panicked, she wanted to pick up as soon as possible, but something seemed to make her hesitate.

劉芷妤
LÂU TSÍ-Û

She cleared her throat, before answering in an unusually high-pitched voice that sounded overly cheerful. Perhaps she was truly overjoyed to receive the call. The man in the window seat frowned and glanced at her.

"Hello, Yinyin? Yeah, I'm already on the train... Has he arrived? Where is he right now?... Alright, I get it, don't be scared, I'll sleep next to you tonight... Of course, I promised you, so I'll be there... Oh go to the living room, turn the TV volume up, then you won't hear anything from their room... Yes, turn the volume all the way up, I'm almost there... If, I said *if* he comes out before I arrive, wait for me at the convenience store in the alley, yes, where I took you to buy ice cream... Alright, I'm almost there, don't be afraid... Remember to bring your phone with you, let me know if anything comes up... You'll be fine... *Don't be scared...*"

Yu-Jie wasn't sure if this was for Yinyin or for herself. She had no confidence in standing up to her sister's new boyfriend and wasn't even sure what her sister would do if such a conflict did arise. After all, it was because her sister wasn't protecting her daughter sufficiently that Yu-Jie had had to put aside her own work, which was already on the edge of a high cliff, to intervene, to stay close to Yinyin.

But then, how can I truly protect her? Yu-Jie thought about her secret consultation a few days ago, in which she had received a simple yet impossible suggestion to "collect evidence first." *But how could I ask a nine-year-old to collect evidence without her mother finding out? How do I protect her in the meantime?*

So, in the end she bought her a mobile phone. She entered her mobile number, Yinyin's school teacher's number, and the emergency line 119. She also taught Yinyin how to record audio and video.

Yu-Jie closed her eyes, the back of her head pressed hard against her seat. She was hoping to squeeze out twenty more years of wisdom for Yinyin. *Is this the best way to go about this?* Like a marquee, her mind span with vicious comments and scenes, messages she had seen on Facebook as she helped the MP respond

别人的孩子
NOT YOUR CHILD

to all the hate — *She has never had a child, what does she know, how dare she do this, how dare she say that?*

Could it be true she loved her niece more than her sister did her own daughter? Could she be more fearful for her safety? What made her want so badly to protect a child who was not her own? And where would this lead — even if everything went smoothly, this might cause her sister to lose custody of — she would lose her boyfriend, Yinyin would lose her mother, their sibling relationship would be torn apart forever. No matter how hard she cared for Yinyin, she would still never be her child. Things were so less certain than every online comment and demand, so less righteous, so messy.

After the train passed Banqiao, it seemed to pick up speed, but it still didn't feel fast enough. Over and over, Yu-Jie checked her phone to make sure she hadn't missed any calls or messages, but there was nothing at all — neither a notification after the office meeting requesting her to draft the final speech, nor a message letting her know the monster was moving from her sister's room to Yinyin's. Yu-Jie wasn't sure whether she should be anxious about the bad signal on the high-speed rail or glad because perhaps no news was good news.

The baby on board began an excruciating howl. The little girl tried to help soothe the baby for her mother but ended up losing patience and scolding it in a high-pitched voice. Her mother then had to intervene, which made her cry as well. There was nothing she could do to calm both of them, so the young mother became helpless as the entire car, in an instant, erupted with judgement and adult wailing.

"Parents these days don't know anything. So noisy and stubborn, but she isn't doing anything about it! People nowadays, huh. Know how to make babies well enough but not how to raise them."

劉芷妤
LÂU TSÍ-Û

"We've also paid for our tickets. We are already standing, can't we at least have some quiet? If the kids are going to be like this the whole time, I'm gonna go crazy. What am I even paying for?"

"Don't have kids if you don't know how to raise them, is it that hard to understand? If they're this loud, why doesn't she ask her husband to drive them? If she can't manage to keep discipline between them, don't bring them out of the house to bother other people."

"Daddy, look at me, I behave so well, not like that little girl, so noisy! Am I a good kid? Can I have an Iron Man? Please! You promised me that if I was good you would buy me one!"

Yu-Jie, who had been barely tolerating the wailing herself, felt even more irritated by the reaction of the others. In need of some kind of distraction, and against her better judgement, she opened the Facebook app on her phone, thinking to perhaps respond to a few messages targeting the MP as any distraction at all was better than this, but, again perhaps because of the speed of the train, the signal was still really bad. The round loading sign just kept spinning a circle, over and over again.

As the train arrived at Taichung station, the loading circle finally stopped. She was about to get back to the messages when, across the corridor, the pair of bobas from earlier began fully bellowing, "Hey, another press conference! Does that old hag even know what she's doing? She's even reeling out someone else's daughter... Oh *please*, this is nothing but a waste of all of our time and money..."

It was like she'd been slapped by a whip — Yu-Jie was in shock and sat bolt-upright. She quickly checked again that there had been no calls or messages on her phone. She exhaled deeply, then called the office.

"Hello? Oh, Yu-Jie, what's up?"

"Hey Jessica, is the meeting over? Any updates?"

别人的孩子
NOT YOUR CHILD

"Oh, just apologies, you know, under such circumstances, it's not the best time to push back, that sort of thing. Public relations is all about resolving people instead of resolving issues, lah…"

"Ok, got it. Could you send me a summary, meeting notes — I can start making a draft?"

"Oh, about that — ummm, actually, Madame Mazu has already asked A-mei to draft it. So all good. They're discussing it right now, actually — and I think they're ready to send it out soon…"

"Um, A-mei? Why her? And is Madame Mazu upset I'm not in the office, do you know?"

"Not really. She's so distracted by everything, I don't think she even noticed. She did say something about how the topic this time, um, needs a bit more compassion, so she asked A-mei, who's a *mother*, to draft her speech, saying that it would be *more convincing*. You know… Just generally, though — like, the public is blaming Madame Mazu for not having *been a mother*, not knowing what it's like to be one, all that, so I guess it makes sense to ask a *mother* to draft her speech…"

It does make sense.

In a blur, Yu-Jie ended the call. The train picked up speed again. The messages that she had sent to Yinyin had bounced back in the meantime, so she re-sent them, but again they failed. She tried again, still nothing. She felt like the passengers on her left and right could smell her thick odour of failure, and if it were not for general courtesy, they might have already pinched their noses and asked her to leave.

By now, Yu-Jie was halfway through her journey and had simply taken to staring at the back of the seat in front of her, trying to restrain herself from locking eyes with any nearby passengers, otherwise she might burst into tears. She couldn't tell why she

劉芷妤
LÂU TSÍ-Û

was going to cry. She hated crying. As a woman, no matter how she cried, it would only show that she was hysterical, that she was looking for attention or otherwise not crying out of true feeling. She couldn't cry, anyway. She had to be strong for Yinyin.

The high-speed rail had just passed Taichung, and she was only halfway to someone else's child, whom she was desperately trying to protect. There was still another half of the journey to go. *Another half.* Why must it be so slow? It was as though she had already travelled twice the distance, such was the difficulty, and yet, at the same time, it felt as though she hadn't made any progress at all.

ká-sióng, from the Taiwanese romanisation of 假想, which means make-believe, imagine, hypothesise — derived from 假/ká meaning 'false' and 想 'sióng' meaning 'thinking', so 'false thinking' / imagination / hypothesis — is the latest series of new translations from Strangers Press, the people who brought you Keshiki and Yeoyu.

This time out we are featuring writers and translators from **Taiwan** in a set of five thrillingly distinctive chapbooks expertly curated in partnership with series editor, Jeremy Tiang, and exquisitely designed with our customary flair. The perfect pick-me-up for the literary curious, each carefully selected story is full of piercing insight and intrigue.

LITERATURE FROM TAIWAN

National Museum of Taiwan Literature

文化部
MINISTRY OF CULTURE, TAIWAN

UEA
University of East Anglia

NORWICH UNIVERSITY OF THE ARTS

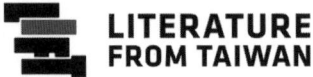

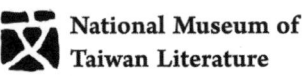

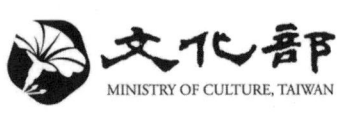

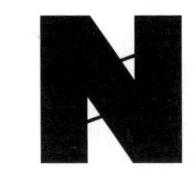

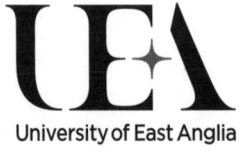